15th February 1990

Jolly Sailor

Mrs Pengelly's

Chapel

Jim Merrymeet's

ALSO BY PAUL ROGERS AND ROBIN BELL CORFIELD

Somebody's Awake
Somebody's Sleepy

For Catherine R.B.C.
For Paul Tavner P.R.

A CIP catalogue record for this book
is available from The British Library.

ISBN 0-370-31204-X

Text copyright © Paul Rogers 1990
Illustrations copyright © Robin Bell Corfield 1990
Printed and bound in Italy for
The Bodley Head Children's Books
20 Vauxhall Bridge Road, London SW1V 2SA
by L.E.G.O., Vicenza, Italy

First published 1990

DON'T BLAME ME!

Paul Rogers

Illustrated by Robin Bell Corfield

The Bodley Head · London

Mr Herring was happy and proud. It was the day of his daughter's wedding. As he came out of the Jolly Sailor, he didn't see Jethro up the ladder. He didn't notice the dribbles of yellow paint.

Soon the sign was shining like new. But just as
Jethro was putting the finishing touches to it...

Captain Crab rushed out, ranting and roaring, and STREAK went the brush, right through Jethro's work. Down came Jethro to give Captain Crab a piece of his mind.

"Don't blame me!" said Captain Crab. "I was having a quiet drink when – what do you think? I saw my boat drift out to sea! That no good goat of Mrs Pengelly's had eaten right through the rope!"

So off Jethro stormed to give Mrs Pengelly a piece of his mind.

"Don't blame me!" said Mrs Pengelly. "I was in the middle of milking when I heard a yell. And there was Dick Trevelyan, dangling from a ledge at the back of the chapel!"

So off Jethro charged to give Dick a piece
of his mind.

"Don't blame me!" said Dick. "I was quietly cleaning windows when Jim Merrymeet's horse, Bessie, whipped the ladder from under me!"

So off Jethro marched to give Jim Merrymeet a piece of his mind.

"Don't blame me!" said Jim. "I was delivering my flowers, when – CRASH – Pip Piper dropped a whole crateful of bottles! It frightened my poor Bessie so bad she made a dash for it."

So off Jethro hurried to give Pip Piper a piece of his mind.

"Don't blame me!" said Pip. "What else could I do, seeing the Braddocks' baby hurtling downhill in its pram, and no one with it!"

So off Jethro stomped to give Mrs Braddock a piece
of his mind.

"Don't blame me!" said Mrs Braddock. "I was pushing Lucy along, when all of a sudden a cake came whizzing towards me! I took my hands off the pram without thinking. It's all the fault of that idiot baker's boy!"

So off Jethro puffed to give the baker's boy a piece
of his mind.

"Don't blame me!" said the baker's boy. "I was pedalling past the Herrings' house with the wedding cake, when suddenly there was a terrible shout and the cat shot out. I slammed on the brakes and the top of the cake just went sailing away."

So off Jethro trudged to give
Mr Herring a piece of his mind.
He had to hunt high and low to
find him.

"Don't blame me!" said Mr Herring. "Wouldn't *you* be upset? I'd just got back from the Jolly Sailor, dressed up for my daughter's wedding, and what did I find? My Sunday-best jacket spattered with yellow paint!"

And off Mr Herring went to the wedding party.

"Yellow paint?" said Jethro. "Floundering flatfish! Then I know who's to blame!"

And feeling ever so foolish, off he went to the Jolly
Sailor, where the bride gave Jethro a piece of her...

wedding cake!

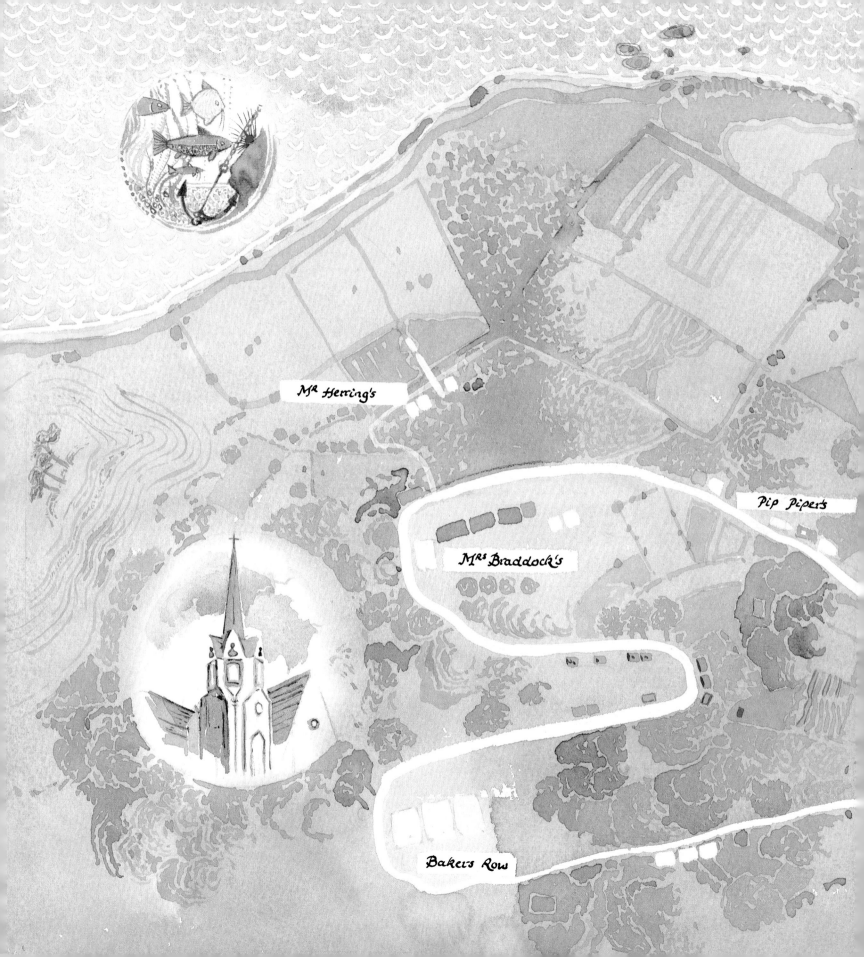

Mr Herring's

Pip Pipers

Mrs Braddock's

Bakers Row